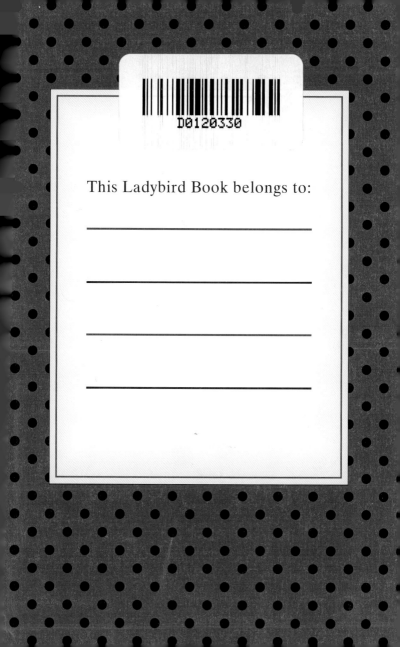

This Ladybird Book belongs to:

_____

_____

_____

_____

Let's read together readers and activity books are designed for you and your child to share.

Miss Polly had a dolly is based on the well-known rhyme, which all children love. The rhyme is given on the left-hand page for the adult to read to the child. On the right-hand page, your child can join in by reading the text given in **bold**. Words from the rhyme are sometimes repeated, and new words are added to tell the story of a doctor's visit!

First read the book aloud. Then go through the rhyme again, this time encouraging your child to read the text on the right-hand page. The illustrations give picture cues to the words. Many young children will remember the words rather than be able to read them, but this is an important part of learning to read. Always praise as you go along – keep your reading sessions fun, and stop if your child loses interest.

Ladybird books are widely available, but in case of difficulty may be ordered by post or telephone from:

Ladybird Books – Cash Sales Department
Littlegate Road Paignton Devon TQ3 3BE
Telephone 01803 554761

A catalogue record for this book is available
from the British Library

Published by Ladybird Books Ltd Loughborough Leicestershire UK
Ladybird Books Inc Auburn Maine 04210 USA

Ladybird

Miss Polly
had a dolly

by Karen Bryant-Mole
illustrated by John Blackman

Miss Polly had a dolly
Who was sick, sick, sick.

Polly

So she phoned the doctor…

Polly's telephone

The doctor came…

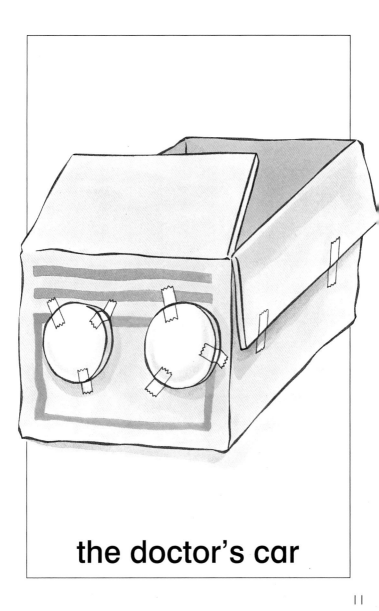

the doctor's car

With his bag ...

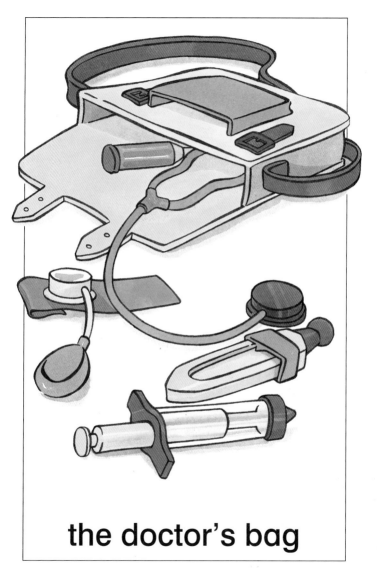

the doctor's bag

And his hat...

the doctor's hat

He looked at the dolly…

Polly's dolly

And he shook his head.

Oh dear!

He said…

23

He wrote on some paper for a pill, pill, pill…

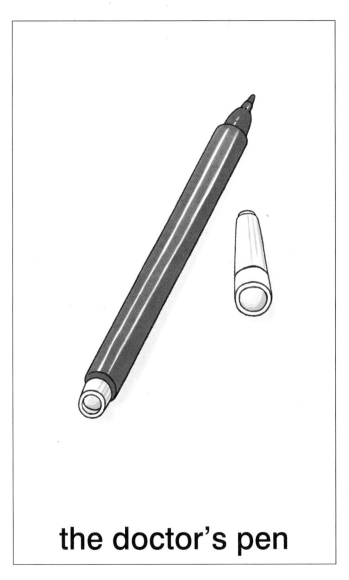

the doctor's pen

I'll be back in the morning with my...